Running Away From Home

For Sam — NG
For Alexander and the Barrys — GR

Grateful acknowledgement is made to the Trustees of the Pooh Properties for the use of WINNIE-THE-POOH and characters based on E.H.Shepard's illustrations, Copyright E.H. Shepard under the Berne Convention and in the USA Copyright © 1926 by E.P.Dutton & Co Inc, Copyright renewed 1954 by A.A.Milne.

A Red Fox Book

Published by Random House Children's Books
20 Vauxhall Bridge Road, London SW1V 2SA

A division of Random House UK Ltd
London Melbourne Sydney Auckland
Johannesburg and agencies throughout the world

Text copyright © 1995 by Nigel Gray
Illustrations copyright © 1995 by Gregory Rogers

3 5 7 9 10 8 6 4 2

First published in Australia by Random House Australia Pty.,
20 Alfred Street, Milsons Point, Sydney, NSW 2061 1995

First published in Great Britain by Andersen Press Ltd 1995

Red Fox edition 1997

Printed in Hong Kong

RANDOM HOUSE UK Limited Reg. No. 954009

ISBN 0 09 972461 8

RUNNING AWAY FROM HOME

STORY BY NIGEL GRAY
PICTURES BY GREGORY ROGERS

Red Fox

ONE SUNDAY AFTERNOON, Sam's dad was being even more bossy and obstreperous than usual. Sam shouted, "I don't want to live with you, ever again! I'm leaving home!"

Sam went into his bedroom, got his school rucksack and tipped all his school things onto the bedroom floor.

He then stuffed into the rucksack: two pairs of shorts; three t-shirts; one pair of pyjama trousers; one pair of underpants; three socks; his *Very First Poetry Book* and *Winnie the Pooh*; a few cars and play people; his recorder; a special piece of wood he had found; his torch (which had no batteries); some batteries (of a different size - batteries always came in handy); his treasure box with its crystals, stones and shells; his bean-bag frog and a bag of marbles.

Sam could hardly lift the rucksack off the ground. He set it down and took out the shorts and t-shirts and pyjama trousers.

Sam got his rucksack onto his back. He tucked his pillow under one arm, and Low Brow under the other.

At the door he stopped, said goodbye to all his friends, looked sadly around the room that he'd lived in all his life, and went out through the living room.

He paused on his way to stroke the dog. He kissed her on the head. "Goodbye, Bella," he said, trying not to cry. Bella thumped the floor with her tail and licked his hand.

"Where are you off to, ragamuffin?" Sam's dad asked.

"I'm going away and I'm never coming back!" said Sam.

Sam went out onto the verandah and let the screen door bang shut behind him. It had been raining on and off all day. Just then, it began to pour.

Sam went down the stairs and stood under the house looking out at the deluge. He was planning to live in the den that he and his big brother, Joe, had built in Whistlepipe Gulley. But it was raining cats and dogs and he didn't want to get Low Brow and his pillow wet.

A wind had sprung up and the trees shimmied and shook like the grass skirts of South Sea Island dancers. The road shone like a stream.

Sam waited for the rain to cease, but it just poured down in a torrent. The rucksack was heavy and the straps were cutting into Sam's shoulders. Sam looked around for somewhere to shelter until the rain stopped, and decided upon Joe's skateboard ramp.

Sam watched the road for
a while. Occasionally a car
hissed by. He could hear a
bird singing. "I don't know
what you've got to sing about,"
Sam said. He took out his
Winnie the Pooh book.

Sam tried to read the story
about Eeyore losing his tail.
But usually Sam's dad read to
him, and Sam found it a
difficult story to read on his
own. Besides, Eeyore was so
sad, and that made Sam sad too.

Sam put his book away and took out his recorder. He lay back on his pillow and played for a while, melancholy music that he made up as he went along.

Above his head he saw a brown spider in its web. Sam waggled the web a little to give the spider a see-saw. The spider scurried off into a dark corner and disappeared.

"Come back, spider," Sam
said. "Please come back." But
the spider didn't come back.

"Now I've got nobody,"
Sam said.

Suddenly the downpour eased
off into a drizzle. Sam decided
it was time to go. He repacked
his rucksack, hoisted it onto his
back, picked up his pillow and
Low Brow — and then
remembered something he'd
forgotten.

He went back up to the house.

"Hi, Sam," said Dad.

"Have you come home, dear?" asked Mum.

"No!" said Sam. Bella jumped up and wagged her tail and licked his arm.

He went to the bathroom and got his new toothbrush (the one shaped like a lady's leg that Joe had given him for Christmas) and slipped it into the pillowcase.

"Would you like a piece of cake before you go?" Dad asked.

"No!" said Sam.

"You don't have to leave home if you don't want to," Mum said.

"I want to," said Sam.

Sam went out onto the verandah. He stood for a while watching the gentle rain washing the world clean. The wind had dropped and the trees had stopped their wild dance. He turned around and went back in.

"I think I will have the piece of cake," he said.

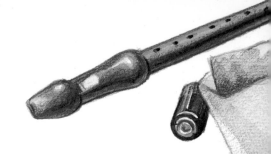

He dumped his things on the floor.
The *Winnie the Pooh* book slid out of
the rucksack onto the rug. Mum gave
him a glass of orange juice and a large
slice of carrot cake.
"Do you want me to read you a story?"
Dad asked.
"OK," said Sam.
"Do you want to sit on my lap?" Dad
asked.
"No," said Sam.

So Sam lay on the rug and heard about how Eeyore lost his tail, but then found it again. Bella came to sit beside Sam and she gave his face a lick.

"She's telling you she's glad you're here," Dad said. "And I'm glad you're here too."

"All right," said Sam. "I'll give you one last chance."

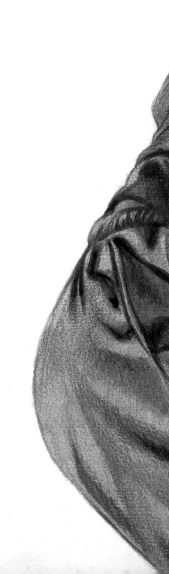